P9-ELW-954

For all the teachers, librarians, and students who
make their schools a welcoming place to learn and grow
—AP & SK

THIS BOOK is inspired by Suzanne's daughters' school, Kimball Elementary, where diversity and community are not just protected, but celebrated. Suzanne created a poster for Kimball teachers to welcome all to their school, and the poster spread to other schools and communities throughout the United States. When Alexandra saw the image, it reminded her of the schools in her community in Brooklyn. She couldn't get the characters out of her mind and one late night sat down to write this story. We hope *All Are Welcome* is a celebration of diversity, and gives encouragement and support to all kids.

THIS IS A BORZOI BOOK PUBLISHED BY ALFRED A. KNOPF

Text copyright © 2018 by Alexandra Penfold
Jacket art and interior illustrations copyright © 2018 by Suzanne Kaufman

All rights reserved. Published in the United States by Alfred A. Knopf, an imprint of Random House Children's Books,
a division of Penguin Random House LLC, New York.

Knopf, Borzoi Books, and the colophon are registered trademarks of Penguin Random House LLC.

Visit us on the Web! rhcbooks.com

Educators and librarians, for a variety of teaching tools, visit us at RHTeachersLibrarians.com

Library of Congress Cataloging-in-Publication Data
Names: Penfold, Alexandra, author. | Kaufman, Suzanne, illustrator.
Title: All are welcome / by Alexandra Penfold ; illustrated by Suzanne Kaufman.
Description: First edition. | New York : Alfred A. Knopf, 2018. |
Summary: Illustrations and simple, rhyming text introduce a school where diversity
is celebrated and songs, stories, and talents are shared.
Identifiers: LCCN 2017027975 (print) | LCCN 2017039593 (ebook) | ISBN 978-0-525-57964-9 (trade) |
ISBN 978-0-525-57965-6 (lib. bdg.) | ISBN 978-0-525-57966-3 (ebook)
Subjects: | CYAC: Stories in rhyme. | Schools—Fiction. | Cultural pluralism—Fiction.
Classification: LCC PZ8.3.P376 (ebook) | LCC PZ8.3.P376 All 2018 (print) | DDC [E]—dc23

The text of this book is set in 16/22-point Corporative Soft.
The illustrations were created using acrylic paint, ink, crayon, and collage with Adobe Photoshop.
Book design by Martha Rago
MANUFACTURED IN CHINA
July 2018
10 9 8 7 6 5 4 3 2 1
First Edition

Random House Children's Books supports the First Amendment and celebrates the right to read.

Alexandra Penfold ☀ Suzanne Kaufman

All Are Welcome

Alfred A. Knopf ⟋ New York

Pencils sharpened in their case.
Bells are ringing, let's make haste.
School's beginning, dreams to chase.

All are welcome here.

No matter how you start your day.
What you wear when you play.

Or if you come from far away.

All are welcome here.

In our classroom safe and sound.
Fears are lost and hope is found.

Raise your hand, we'll go around.

All are welcome here.

Gather now, let's all take part.
We'll play music, we'll make art.

We'll share stories from the heart.

All are welcome here.

Time for lunch—what a spread!
A dozen different kinds of bread.
Pass it around till everyone's fed.

All are welcome here.

Open doors, rush outside.
We will swing, we will slide.
We'll have fun side by side.

All are welcome here.

We're part of a community.
Our strength is our diversity.
A shelter from adversity.

All are welcome here.

We will learn from each other.
Special talents we'll uncover.

There's a big world to discover.

All are welcome here.

So much to learn, so much to do.
And when the busy day is through,

Can't wait to come back, start anew.

All are welcome here.

Head for home to get some rest

and greet tomorrow, ready and fresh.

Our time together is the best.

All are welcome here.

You are welcome here.

You have a place here.

You have a space here.